MEET THE GIRL TALK CHARACTERS

Sabrina Wells is petite, with curly auburn hair, sparkling hazel eyes, and a bubbly personality. Sabrina loves magazines, shopping, sleepovers, and most of all, she loves talking to her best friends.

Katie Campbell is a straight-A student and super athlete. With her blond hair, blue eyes, and matching clothes, she's everyone's idea of little miss perfect. But Katie has a few surprises for everyone, including herself!

Randy Zak has just moved to Acorn Falls from New York City, and is she ever cool! With her "radical" spiked haircut and her hip New York clothes, Randy teaches everyone just how much fun it is to be different.

Allison Cloud is a Native American Indian. Allison's super smart and really beautiful. But she has one major problem: She's thirteen years old, five foot seven, and still growing!

Here's what they're talking about in
Girl Talk

SABRINA: Scottie Silver may be gorgeous, but he seems like a real jerk.

KATIE: Oh, I don't know, he's not so bad.

SABRINA: After what he did to you today?

KATIE: Actually, if you think about it, he was trying to help me out.

SABRINA: Well, I never thought it would happen to Katie Campbell!

KATIE: Sabs, what are you talking about?

SABRINA: Oh, nothing — except your crush on Scottie Silver, eighth-grade hunk and captain of the hockey team — that's all!

FACE-OFF!

By L. E. Blair

GIRL TALK® series created by Western Publishing Company, Inc.

Produced by Angel Entertainment, Inc.

Western Publishing Company, Inc., Racine, Wisconsin 53404

Text by Cathy Lasry

Chapter One

Princess Emily. That's what I call my older sister, Emily, but never out loud, only to myself. Don't get me wrong. It's not that I don't like having a sister who is beautiful, captain of the varsity pom-pom squad, a straight-A student, and also going out with the star quarterback of the Bradley High School football team. It's just that she's a lot to live up to — and even more to live with.

That's why when my best friend, Sabrina, mentioned that Emily was on the other side of the ice-skating rink with her boyfriend, Reed, I got really mad. "Sabs, if you don't stop going on and on about Emily, I'll..." I was so annoyed that I couldn't think of anything to say.

Sometimes it bothers me that Sabrina finds Emily so wonderful. I think it's because Sabs only has brothers. She has four of them, actually, including a twin named Sam.

Anyway, Sabs (which is one of Sabrina's nicknames) was just standing there looking really hurt that I'd yelled at her. "I'm sorry, Sabs," I finally said.

She grinned and said, "Forget it. It's okay." Sabs is like that. She never stays mad at anybody. I had to crack a smile.

While I was lacing up my skates, Randy Zak came walking over to us. Next to her, I feel a little like Miss Goody Two-Shoes. Personally, I think Randy is the coolest dresser I've ever seen. I just can't imagine my ever daring to wear the kind of clothes that she does, but they look great on her.

Today Randy was decked out in what Sabs calls her "Downtown New York" look. She was wearing zebra-striped leggings, a black-and-white miniskirt, and this big neon-green sweater that kept falling off her shoulders. She also had on one big neon-green hoop earring in her left ear and three small gold hoop earrings in her right ear.

On the other hand, I was wearing jeans that my mother had insisted on ironing, a light blue sweater with white snowflakes around the collar, and a matching snowflake hat. Forget the earrings. I'm not allowed to get my ears pierced until I turn sixteen, and even then I'll probably only be allowed to wear little gold balls or pearls or something like that. Anyway, I probably wouldn't dress like Randy, even if I could. As Sabs would say, I have my own style.

"So, what's up?" Randy asked with a sort of bored expression on her face.

Randy's parents are divorced, and she moved here to Acorn Falls with her mother at the beginning of the school year. After New York City, I think Randy finds Acorn Falls a little boring. At first I thought she was obnoxious and had an attitude problem, but then I realized that she's actually quite nice.

"I'm going skating," I said, getting up. "You guys coming?"

"Nope," said Randy. "I have to go soon. My mother wants to go shopping for clothes."

Sabs just laughed. She hates to skate, but she goes to the rink because everyone hangs out there and she doesn't want to miss anything. Randy doesn't know how to ice-skate. She claims she only comes by because there isn't anything else to do.

"Well, catch you guys later," I called to them

and headed toward the ice. Skating is just about my favorite thing in the world. I took a moment to look around. The rink was really crowded. Besides Emily and Reed, I'd say most of the kids from the high school and a big group of eighth-graders were there. Lots of seventh-graders like Sabs, Randy, and me hang out at the new rink, too.

The town built this indoor rink about two years ago. It has a snack bar and tables and lockers to put all your stuff in. It is a great place to hang out, I have to admit.

Everybody used to skate at the school's hockey rink, or at Elm Park. I love Elm Park. It's really nice with the trees and the grass, and no fence around the ice. But everyone loves to hang out around the high school kids at the new rink. I kind of miss Elm Park, though. It's where I used to skate with my dad when I was little.

I got out onto the ice, and it felt great. It was really hard and smooth, like glass. I managed to find a clear spot over toward the left of the rink, and I began to practice some figure-skating moves. I was trying to do this cool move I'd seen on the international figure-skating competitions on TV. It's called a flying camel. It wasn't easy to do, and I felt a little self-conscious, but I was determined to get the hang of it.

Finally the move seemed more natural and I began twirling to the music playing on the loudspeaker. It was the kind of music that makes my mother tap her foot and hum. You know, the kind of music that makes you feel like getting a pair of earplugs. You'd think they'd have better music, considering that so many kids hang out at the rink. Anyway, this music had a catchy beat, and I really started getting into what I was doing.

"I didn't know you could skate like that," somebody crooned behind my back. I came to a stop and turned around. It was Stacy the Great.

Stacy is not only the most popular girl in junior high school, she also happens to be the principal's daughter. Stacy, Sabrina, Randy, and I all go to the same school, Bradley Junior High.

Stacy's an only child, and everyone knows that her parents spoil her rotten, especially her mother. Stacy has incredible clothes and jewelry, and, of course, she's beautiful. She has waist-length, wavy blond hair and big brown eyes. She has a great figure and has never had a pimple in her life. She's also on the flag squad like I am, but she's the seventh-grade flag captain.

Today she was wearing a pale yellow skating skirt with a matching turtleneck sweater, and these diamond stud earrings that sparkled in the light. My mom has diamond earrings, but she only wears them when she gets dressed up to go out. I couldn't imagine myself wearing diamond earrings to go skating. But that's Stacy.

Anyway, I don't understand what Stacy is up to lately. Ever since my best friend, Erica, moved to California, Stacy's been acting really odd. Erica and Stacy were pretty good friends, so Stacy let me hang out with her crowd last year. But since Erica left, Stacy hasn't seen any reason to be friendly to me. And now that I've made friends with Sabrina and Randy, she's totally ignored me.

Stacy gets along with Randy and Sabs like fire and water. It's obvious that Stacy is jealous of Sabrina because she has so many friends. Then, in the beginning of the year, when Sabs got a special spotlight dance at the homecoming party, Stacy was really furious. And forget about Stacy and Randy. On Randy's first day of school here she "accidentally" dumped Stacy's entire trayful of disgusting school food all over Stacy's clothes. Stacy got really mad, especially when everybody in the cafeteria laughed.

So I wondered why Stacy was suddenly talking to me. I guess she wanted to look really popular and talk to a lot of people.

"I'm just practicing some moves I learned in my skating lessons," I finally said. But I didn't really smile at her or anything.

"Hey!" Stacy suddenly grabbed my arm.

I almost jumped out of my skates.

"Scottie Silver's over there. Let's go," Stacy whispered and skated away.

I wasn't about to follow Stacy, but I did look over in Scottie Silver's direction. Scottie is definitely cute, and he definitely knows it. He has thick blond hair that's a little long in the back and curls up around his sweater collar, and the most gorgeous blue eyes I've ever seen. When he smiles, his eyes sort of crinkle up and you can see his dimples. He's also really tall and broad-shouldered, and he looks great in his jeans and orange-and-black hockey letter jacket. It was obvious Stacy had a big crush on him. They'd look great together, no doubt about it.

I didn't want to waste my whole afternoon gawking, and all of that exercise had given me a huge appetite, so I skated off the ice and went over to the snack bar. Having a snack bar at the rink was a great idea. I got two candy bars and a Coke and went to join Allison Cloud, another member of my new group, and Sabs. They were at the other end of the rink, sitting at one of the long wooden picnic tables. All of the tables close to the snack bar were completely packed. Those benches have belonged to the high school kids ever since the rink opened, and it was lucky that Sabs and Al had found us some seats. I saw Emily sitting with some of her friends. She waved at me and I waved back, but I hurried over to Sabs and Allison before I lost my seat.

"Al, tell Katie what you just told me," Sabs began even before I had a chance to sit down. "Go on, Al, tell her," she continued excitedly.

This had to be about a guy. Sabs always gets hyper when she talks about guys. Her hazel eyes sparkled, and she kept pushing her curly auburn hair off her face. Sabs has really gorgeous hair. She took a French fry and popped it into her mouth. So much for her latest diet. She's always trying to lose a few pounds. Sabs says she has a lot of baby fat, but she looks perfectly fine to me. Right now she was excited, and whenever Sabs gets excited about something, she eats. That happens about every ten seconds.

I looked at Allison and smiled. She's the exact opposite of Sabs in almost every way. While Sabs is a chatterbox, Allison is quiet and shy. Al notices things about people that I would never see in a million years. Allison also looks like a model, but I don't think she knows it. She's a Native American Indian and has incredible dark brown eyes and long, long, thick, shiny black hair. She's also really tall. She's five foot seven and still growing. She's not exactly thrilled about her height, but Sabs and I both think she's really lucky to be so tall. It's really funny to see Al and Sabs together since Sabs is kind of on the short side.

Allison didn't look like she was too excited about telling me this big news, so I decided to change the subject.

"By the way," I said, taking a slow sip of

Coke, "where's Randy?" I looked around. I knew I was driving Sabs crazy. She was obviously dying to tell me this big news, and I was acting as if I didn't care.

"Katie..." Sabs said.

"Okay, okay," I finally said, giving in. "What is it?"

Naturally, Sabs couldn't wait for Allison to tell me. "Al said she saw Scottie Silver watching you while you were twirling around out there," Sabs said quickly, in her usual breathless way.

I tried to act really cool about what she'd just said, but actually I felt like falling off the bench. I looked over at the girls sitting next to us. I hoped they weren't listening to our conversation. I was already embarrassed. "Sabs, would you please lower your voice?" I asked in a loud whisper. Anyway, Scottie Silver, eighth-grade hunk and captain of the hockey team, would never notice *me*. Especially with Stacy the Great falling all over him.

"He was probably just looking in my direction," I finally said, trying to brush it off. "Or maybe he was watching my skating, since he's such a good skater." I bit into one of my chocolate bars and looked over at Scottie. He was sitting at a table closer to the snack bar with Stacy and her clique, along with two guys from the hockey team, Phil Walsh and Brian Williams. They were all laughing and Brian was throwing candy at Eva Malone, one of Stacy the Great's clones, who kept shrieking and then throwing them back at him. Scottie and Stacy were sharing a bag of potato chips.

"Look at the way Stacy's acting around Scottie. He's eating it up," Sabs continued with a sigh.

I tried not to think about it, but every time I looked in Scottie's direction, I got really embarrassed. "I think I'm going to go skating again. Wanna come?" I looked at Sabs and Allison.

"Sure," said Allison.

"I better go," Sabs replied. "If I don't get that paper finished for English, I'll have to write another poem and read it in front of the whole class again. That's worse than detention, believe me."

We said good-bye to Sabs, then Allison and I walked out toward the rink. Suddenly somebody zoomed up behind me, pulled off my hat, and sped away. It was Scottie Silver. I didn't even stop to think; I just took off after him. We raced around the rink, dodging kids, and almost knocking some of them over. I didn't know if anybody was watching because everything was a blur as I whirled around the rink.

After our first time around the rink, Scottie was still a little ahead of me, so I picked up speed. But I still couldn't catch him — he'd had a head start, after all. Then just as he was making a wide turn around the middle of the rink, I caught up to him and grabbed him by one of his belt loops. One of his blades got stuck in the ice, though, and as he stuck out his arms trying to regain his balance, he knocked into a girl and a guy skating right ahead of him. The next thing I knew, we were all lying in a big heap on the ice.

Scottie was lying on his back, and I was lying facedown next to him. The two people we had knocked down started to get mad.

"Sorry about that," I apologized to them as I stood up. I was really embarrassed. I could feel myself blushing.

They just skated off. Scottie didn't say anything at all. He just grinned at me, wiped off his pants, and skated off the ice to where Stacy and her group were standing.

"Are you okay?" Allison asked as she came skating up to me.

"Yeah, I'm fine," I replied quickly. Actually, I felt a little sore, and my left knee had started bleeding, but I was more shaken up by what Scottie had done than by anything else.

When Allison and I got to the lockers, Stacy came over to us. She'd already changed into her shoes. I guess she just couldn't resist giving me a jab before the day was over.

"Katie, you chase after boys almost as well as you skate," Stacy said in her most obnoxious voice.

I just stood there and blushed. I couldn't think of anything to say. Stacy obviously wanted-ed to embarrass me, and she definitely had succeeded. I finished putting my shoes on and stood up, ignoring her. "Ready?" I asked Allison.

She nodded.

We walked part of the way home together. Fall is my favorite time of year. The air was really cool and crisp and had that smell of burning fireplace logs. I pulled my sweater sleeves down over my hands. Acorn Falls looked beautiful, too, covered with a blanket of red and gold leaves. We walked down Main Street past the old brick post office, the library with the huge oak tree in front, some small stores, and the First National Bank, where my mother works.

"Can you believe it's almost Thanksgiving? It seems like school just started," I said, looking at all of the Thanksgiving decorations in the store windows.

"I know what you mean," Allison replied, shaking her head.

"Katie," Allison began softly, "you really are a fast skater. I think you might even be faster than Scottie."

I just looked at her. I've always loved skating ever since I was little. My father had been a semipro hockey player, and he'd taught me to skate. He'd also taught me how to play hockey and skate fast. Three years ago, when I was ten, I'd been a real demon on the ice. But Mom never let me play after that. Actually, that was right after my father died. She didn't think it was right for a girl to play ice hockey. Being a flag girl and then maybe a cheerleader or a pom-pom girl was about as wild as she wanted me to get.

"Thanks for saying so," I said to Al. "Even if it isn't true."

She just shrugged. "See you tomorrow," she called and she turned down her street.

I walked slowly toward my house, scuffing my sneakers through the leaves. I couldn't stop thinking about Scottie Silver and what happened at the rink. Just thinking about it made my stomach all fluttery, like something special was about to happen.

Chapter Two

I opened the white gate and ran up the front path to my house. Our house is probably the only house in Acorn Falls that doesn't have any leaves on the lawn. My mother is a neat freak. Our house isn't big or anything, but it's always very clean. Everything has its place. I noticed that most of the fall flowers in Mom's garden had bloomed. Gardening is one of my mother's passions. I guess she is pretty good at it because we always have the most beautiful flowers in the neighborhood.

I pulled my keys out of my backpack and went into the house. When I got inside, Emily was setting the table for dinner. She was wearing a pair of pink leggings and a cropped purple sweatshirt, and she had her hair in a high ponytail with a purple-and-pink headband going around her forehead. I must admit that even when my sister was casually dressed, she looked beautiful. Like me, she has blond hair that's almost yellow and big sky-blue eyes. The only difference is, Emily's hair goes almost to her waist. Her nose is perfectly straight and turns up a little at the end. Even her chin is perfect — not too pointy, not too round. Sabs thinks she looks like a Barbie doll. Secretly, I think so, too.

I said hi to Emily and put my skates into the big trunk by the door and got out of my sweater.

"Hi, Katie," Emily replied and finished setting the table.

Soon Mom came downstairs and we all sat down to dinner. We were having spaghetti, one of my favorites, but I was still too excited to eat after everything that had happened at the rink.

"So, how was skating?" Mom asked us.

"Okay," I said quickly, and before I could help myself, I blushed.

"Only okay?" Emily said in this teasing voice. "I'd say you had a pretty interesting afternoon."

"What's that supposed to mean?" I asked.

"Well, I saw you chase that gorgeous little Scottie Silver around the ice. I didn't even know you liked boys, Katie."

Mom and Emily both looked at me. I was too embarrassed to say a word. All I could do was blush. How could Emily tease me like this? It really wasn't funny, especially since Mom has this thing about ladylike behavior. Chasing boys around a rink is definitely not ladylike. Even I know that.

"Emily," I finally said weakly, "you were there. You saw he was the one who started it. And, anyway, we were just having fun."

"Katie," my mother finally said, "I don't mind your having fun, but please be careful. You're a young lady now, and a young lady shouldn't act too rough with boys. I'm sure you don't want them to get the wrong idea."

I shook my head. "I'll be careful," I mumbled. I wasn't sure what Mom meant about wrong ideas, but I just let it go. Besides, I couldn't believe Emily had said anything in the first place. I pushed my spaghetti around my plate with my fork without saying another word.

The next morning I lay in bed for a few extra minutes and just looked around my room. My wallpaper has little rosebuds all over it and it's really faded. I remember when I was six and came home from my first day of first grade, this new wallpaper was up and there were these pink gingham tie-back curtains with lace trim that Mom had made for me on her sewing machine.

My room is very cozy. All my furniture is white with gold trim. The carpet is pale blue and very soft, and it matches the pale blue flowers on my bedspread. And I have a whole matching white wall unit filled with my books and stuffed animals. In the corner is the big white dollhouse my dad made for me when I was little. It even has lights that turn on and off and little tiny curtains at the windows. I know I'm too old for it now, but I still like it.

I got up and took my flag girl uniform out of my closet and laid it out on top of my bed. The uniform is just about the only good thing about being on the flag squad. It's a short orange-and-black-plaid kilt with a matching plaid sash. Being a flag girl is okay, but I'm really doing it because it makes Mom and Emily so happy.

My cat, Pepper, came up to me and rubbed

against my leg. I gave her a big kiss on the head, and then I trudged across the hall to the bathroom. The door was closed. That meant Princess Emily was still in there.

"Come on, Emily, I'm going to be late for school!" I said as I banged on the door. But I knew it wouldn't make any difference. Emily only comes out when she's good and ready. Unfortunately, it's the only bathroom in the house.

I made it to school on time, thank goodness. My first two classes, math and social studies, went pretty quickly. I had a quiz in math I was pretty sure I did okay on. In social studies we watched this boring movie about the Second Continental Congress. Then it was time for English and homeroom. I slid into my seat and looked around for Sabs. I didn't see her anywhere.

Sabs came in five minutes late, walked quickly to the back of the room, and slid into her seat. I knew she was trying to get my attention. She was being pretty obvious about it. Subtle is just not Sabs's style. She was waving her hand and calling my name in a loud whisper. I was looking straight ahead. I didn't want to start passing notes with her and risk getting caught. But then Ms. Staats said without even looking up, "Sabrina, is there something you would like to share with the rest of the class?" Teachers must be mind readers. They always seem to know what's going on.

"No," Sabs finally replied. And I knew without having to turn around that she was probably bright red. Sabs blushes all the time.

Finally the bell rang, and Sabs was at my desk before I could even stand up. Randy and Allison are also in my homeroom, and they came over to my desk, too.

"So what happened yesterday?" Sabs asked excitedly. "I can't believe I missed it. I always miss everything!" she moaned.

"Who are you kidding?" said Randy, laughing. "You never miss a thing. It's like you've got a radar."

I tried not to smile, while Sabs proceeded to give Randy a drop-dead look.

As we walked toward our lockers, I told Sabs a short version of what had happened. But I said everything really softly, since I didn't want any of the other kids to overhear.

"Wow!" Sabs exclaimed. "This is so cool. I

want to hear absolutely every detail."

I just kind of nodded. "Ready to go to lunch?" I asked her.

"I can't," Sabs replied. "I have to meet with Mr. Metcalf and go over my clarinet solo for the Fall Festival concert. But I'll call you tonight," she said just as the warning bell rang.

"You can call me," I replied, "but there really isn't anything to tell, honest. It's no big deal," I added.

Sabs just gave me this all-knowing grin. "Oh, Katie," she said. "I just know there's got to be more. I'll talk to you later." She took off down the hall, almost knocking a teacher down.

Randy, Allison, and I walked out to our favorite spot on the front lawn of the school. We like to eat lunch on the lawn when the weather's good. Lots of kids hang out there, and there are always some teachers around to make sure that we behave ourselves and don't leave the school grounds.

It was actually kind of cold out, but it felt good after being cooped up all morning. I saw Randy stretched out on the grass, facing the sun. Randy absolutely hates cold weather. It must be cold in New York now, too, it's different. I wonder how she's going once winter hits Acorn Falls and every layers on the long underwear, sweaters, a down jackets. It's just hard to picture Randy in a down jacket.

I took my peanut butter and jelly sandwich out of my sandwich bag. Randy always teases me for eating peanut butter and jelly, but I just can't give it up. I only let myself have it two times a week, though.

"It's really nice out," Allison said, briefly looking up from her book.

"Hey," said Randy, "I'm sorry I missed your performance at the rink yesterday. I should have stuck around."

"You really should have," Allison agreed, putting her book down and taking her tuna fish sandwich out of her backpack. "Katie was great! She skates so fast."

"Yeah?" asked Randy. "Well, Katie, maybe you could teach me how to skate sometime. I mean," she added quickly, "if I'm going to have to live here all winter, I might as well learn to ice-skate."

I almost fainted. Randy wanted me to teach

t a couple of weeks
e working on a social
her, Mr. Grey, who's
king, wanted us to do
t the American Revo-
ed to be partners.

e really smart and cre-
of the year, when Sabs,
Allison, Randy, and I were on the homecoming
dance decorating committee, Randy saved the
day. She set up all these high-tech lights, and
when she finished, the gym looked kind of like
a spaceship, which was perfect, because the
theme was Lost in Space.

So for the social studies project we decided
to make a model of the Boston Tea Party. We
found this big piece of wood in my basement
that was perfect for the base of the model. The
only problem was that it was too long and we
had to cut it. Randy claimed that using a saw
was a piece of cake, and she wouldn't let me
give her any directions. So she put the wood on
top of this thin coffee table in our rec room and
started sawing it in half. When she finished
sawing and picked it up, the coffee table broke
in half!

At first we both laughed so hard, I thought my sides were going to split. Then I got really upset. I knew my mom was going to be mad about the table. But Randy was so cool about it. She marched right up to my mom and told her what had happened and how she'd misjudged the measurements and all. Randy offered to go out and buy a new table right then and there, but Mom said she'd rather have us do chores around the house instead. Randy and I had a pretty good time straightening out our garage and basement. That's when I realized she was really okay.

"Katie!" Randy said loudly, breaking into my thoughts and bringing me back to the present.

"Oh, yeah," I replied. "I'll be glad to teach you to skate."

"Isn't that Scottie Silver over there?" Allison asked me, with this little smile on her face.

Sure enough, it was. Scottie was walking down the front steps with his usual gang of friends, mostly eighth-grade jocks, including Brian Williams and Phil Walsh, whom everybody calls Flip. They were all wearing letter jackets and jeans, but Scottie was by far the best-looking. He was talking and waving his arms around, and the other guys were laughing and slapping him on the back.

I turned around and shrugged. "Yeah, so what?" I said. What did they think? That I liked him or something? Great. Now that Allison pointed him out to me, I sat there for the rest of the period wondering if he'd seen me, and if he was going to come over and say anything to me.

But, of course, by the time the bell rang, he hadn't come over. I sneaked a glance in his direction when I stood up to go back into school, but he'd left.

The afternoon passed pretty quickly. The next thing I knew, it was three o'clock and time for flag practice. I really didn't want to go, but I had to. It wouldn't have been right to just not show up, so I put my jacket in my regular locker and went down to the gym.

In the gym locker room, I changed into my uniform and headed out to the field. It wasn't that I had anything against being a flag girl. It is kind of nice to go out there and cheer the team on and get everybody into the school spirit. I just didn't love it, and besides, the only other seventh graders I knew were Stacy and Eva. I'd tried out for the squad with my best friend, Erica, and when she moved away, it just didn't seem as much fun. If it wasn't for Mom and Emily wanting me to be on the squad so badly, I probably wouldn't have stayed on the squad after Erica moved.

Stacy was standing there, smiling and jumping around. But when she spotted me coming in late, her expression changed. I was a few feet from the rest of the squad, and I had a big knot in my stomach. It's bad enough to have to practice with these girls who I feel so uncomfortable around, but I could tell that Stacy was about to say something to embarrass me in front of them.

I tried to concentrate on our routines, but I had trouble remembering what we were supposed to be doing. I guess that's what happens when your heart isn't in something. We started this one routine that's pretty basic but I guess I wasn't trying too hard and I really messed it up. We were supposed to kick our left legs up and then do a turn to the right. Well, I kicked my left leg up, but then I did a turn to the left and I hit this girl named Julie in the face.

"Are you okay?" I asked, going over to her.

Stacy and some of the other girls crowded around her. I felt like turning around and running, but I was glued to the spot.

My heart was racing. I was too scared to even cry. Luckily, I could see Julie was fine. She didn't even have a red mark on her face or anything.

"I'm okay, Katie," Julie said. "Really."

Mrs. O'Neal, the gym teacher, came over then. She asked Julie if she wanted to go to the nurse, but Julie said no, she was okay.

I just sort of stood at the back of the group for the rest of practice. I wasn't exactly the most enthusiastic flag girl, but nobody said anything, not even Stacy. It was a relief when Mrs. O'Neal told us it was time to go.

I got back to the locker room first, and I started getting out of my uniform. I was standing there in my underwear and my white undershirt when everybody else came straggling in. Some of the girls in our grade wear bras, including Stacy the Great, of course, but most of them don't exactly have anything to hold up. I don't need one yet, and from the look of things I won't until I'm about thirty.

Honestly, I've never really thought about the whole thing very much. I kind of like the undershirts. They're really soft and they keep my sweaters from scratching me. They also keep me warmer in the winter. So, like I said, I was standing there in my undershirt when Stacy walked in.

"What a cute little undershirt, Katie," Stacy said in this sugary-sweet voice.

All of the other girls turned to look at me as they made their way to their lockers. I pulled my clothes out of my locker and continued getting dressed, trying to act as if I was ignoring Stacy and everybody else.

"Really, Katie," Eva joined in. "The rest of us gave those up in second grade. I guess you just can't find a bra small enough to fit you!"

She and Stacy and some other girls started to giggle.

That was it. I mean, I'd tried to ignore them, but this was just too much. I could feel the tears welling up in my eyes, but I wasn't about to give them the satisfaction of seeing me cry. I held the tears back and finished getting dressed really quickly, grabbed my books, and ran to Mrs. O'Neal's office. I didn't even bother knocking on her door. I just went in, handed her my uniform, and ran out. I knew that if I tried to say anything, she'd be able to tell I was about to cry.

"Katie!" I could hear Mrs. O'Neal yelling down the hall. "What is this supposed to mean?"

I turned around for a second. "It means I quit!" I shouted back. I couldn't help it. Then I ran out the front door and burst into tears.

Chapter Three

With tears streaming down my face, I ran down the school steps. I kept wiping the tears out of my eyes, but I couldn't stop, and my vision was all blurry. I couldn't believe I'd just gone and thrown my uniform at Mrs. O'Neal, screaming, "I quit." What had come over me?

Now that I'd actually quit, I started to panic. I could only imagine what Mom and Emily would have to say. Thinking about that made me feel even worse, but at least I'd stopped crying. Walking in the cold air also helped clear my head and calm me down.

When I got home, only the porch light and a light in Emily's room were on. Then I remembered that Mom had a late meeting at the bank. She probably wouldn't be home until after eight. Good. I could get in bed and pretend to be sleeping by the time she got home.

I fished my keys out of my backpack, and

opened the door. I dropped my knapsack down on the bench. I could hear Emily in her bedroom exercising to one of those stupid exercise tapes. She looks so ridiculous jumping around in front of the mirror like that. Sometimes I peek in and she's making these really goofy faces, like she's pretending to be Miss America or something.

I walked past the living room, past the small staircase leading upstairs to the bedrooms, and into the kitchen. I like our kitchen a lot, except for the wallpaper. It's got these big yellow daisies all over it. It's also the kind you can wash off. Mom thinks it's practical. Personally, I think it's ugly, but I hardly even notice it anymore. There's one window above the sink with yellow dotted-swiss tie-back curtains. Next to the window is the back door. They both look out over our little yard. When I say little, I mean little. There's barely enough room for the swing set that still sits out there. It's funny that Mom has never gotten rid of it, since we haven't used it for years. I mean, she's always so neat and tidy about everything.

Anyway, right in the middle of the kitchen is a round table made out of this dark, knotty wood with four chairs made out of the same wood around it. There was a note from Mom sitting right in the middle, propped up against the salt shaker.

Katie and Emily,
Made your favorite — lasagna!
Have a good dinner.
Love,
Mom

Now I felt even worse. Mom had gone to a lot of trouble to make the lasagna, and here I was letting her down by not being a flag girl. I popped the lasagna into the oven and made a salad while I watched TV. Mom hates it when I do that, but it relaxes me. When the oven timer rang, I called Emily to dinner.

Part of me wanted to tell Emily I had quit the flag squad, but part of me didn't. I wasn't in the mood for one of Emily's lectures and sisterly advice. Anyway, I knew she was working on some big school project and I didn't want to bother her. As a matter of fact, she gobbled her food down and ran back upstairs to her room.

After dinner, I still felt upset, so I took a pint

of pistachio ice cream out of the freezer. Ice cream sometimes helps to cheer me up.

Before I even had a chance to get a spoon out of the drawer, the phone rang. It's on the wall right next to the kitchen door. I sighed, turned around, and went to pick it up. Emily was already on the line. I could tell it was her boyfriend, Reed, by the way she was laughing and talking all lovey-dovey. Yuck!

I went upstairs to my room and shut the door. Pepper was asleep on my bed. When she heard me come in, she opened her eyes slowly and turned over on her back. She loves to be tickled on her stomach. I tickled her for a few seconds, and then I went over to my bookcase. I have a lot of books, mostly about animals, and I have them all arranged in alphabetical order. I looked them over, but I just wasn't in the mood for any of them.

On the bottom shelf, arranged in order of the date, were all my copies of *Young Chic*. I picked up the most recent issue, stretched out on my bed, and started to flip through it. I really wasn't in the mood for stuff like "Six boys let loose their deepest, darkest fears about girls and dating," or "The right shoes to wear when your feet are growing faster than the rest of you." The articles reminded me of Sabrina.

I decided to call Sabs. I had promised to talk to her, and I wanted to be off the phone and in bed by the time Mom got home. I knocked on Emily's door. She opened it and handed me the phone.

"How did you know what I wanted?" I asked, surprised.

She just shrugged and went over to her desk.

I took the phone into my room. It had an extra-long cord that Emily bought, since Mom wouldn't let either of us have an extension in our rooms. I sat down at my little white desk with the gold trim painted at the edges. It's right in front of my window, which faces toward the front of the house. I like my desk. Everything in it is arranged in just the right way, and I even have different colored folders to put all of my papers and letters and cards in and stuff.

I dialed Sabs's number.

"Yeah?" somebody said instead of "Hello." It was Sam, Sabs's twin, who is older than her by all of four minutes. Sabs is always getting mad at him. They have a real love/hate relationship. I like him a lot, even if I don't like him the way I thought I did at the beginning of the year. Now we're just friends. Sam's actually very cute. He has thick dark red hair, tons of freckles, and adorable big gray eyes. He looks like a boy version of Sabs, although she'd never admit that.

"Hi, Sam. It's me, Katie," I said.

"Hi, Katie. How're you doing? Hold on, I'll get Blabs for you," Sam said.

I giggled. Actually, "Blabs" isn't a bad nickname for her, or for Sam either, since they both talk so much and ask questions without waiting for the answers.

"Hello," Sabs finally said.

"Hi," I said. "Listen, I'm really glad you're there. You won't believe what happened today."

"Was it bad? I knew something bad would happen to you today. I just happened to look at your horoscope this morning, and if you'd asked me, I would have told you to just stay in bed. You see —"

"Sabs!" I interrupted her. She's really into horoscopes, but I don't believe in them. I mean, how can your birthday and the positions of some moons tell you anything about your life?

"Okay," she said. "What happened? Did you see Scottie Silver today? What did he say?"

"No, it's nothing like that," I said. "I quit flag."

"You what?" she yelled. "I can't believe it! Why? I mean, I got the feeling you didn't love it, but I never thought you'd quit. What did your mother and Emily say? Did you tell them yet? What happened? Tell me!"

"Okay, okay," I said. "I don't know how you can talk so fast and ask so many questions in one breath."

Sabs laughed. "I'm just talented, I guess."

"Ha, ha," I said. "Actually, I haven't told my mother yet. She's still at work."

"Oh. So, why'd you do it?" Sabs asked.

"I don't know," I said slowly. "I was just sort of sick of it, you know."

"What? That's why you suddenly decided to quit?" Sabs asked.

"How do you know it was suddenly?" I asked.

"Because you didn't mention anything to *me* about it," she said. "I mean, that is something you'd tell your best friend, isn't it?"

She had me there. But I really didn't feel like getting into the whole story about Stacy and the undershirt, just then. I guess I was too embarrassed about it to even tell Sabs.

"I guess I just forgot," I said. "And, anyway, we didn't have lunch together. As a matter of fact, I haven't seen you since homeroom."

"Yeah," Sabs said. "But still."

"Katie!" I suddenly heard Emily yelling.

"Hold on, Sabs," I said. I put my hand over the receiver. "What do you want?" I yelled back.

"Katie, I'm going to hang this animal out the window if you don't get it out of my room right now!" Emily screamed.

I sighed. "Gotta go, Sabs," I said into the phone. "See you tomorrow."

"Okay, bye," she said. "But I want to hear the details tomorrow."

I hung up the phone and went across the hall to Emily's room. Emily absolutely hates my cat, but for some reason Pepper is always rubbing against her or trying to curl up in her bed. Emily refuses to pick her up, so she always makes me stop whatever I'm doing to deal with her. It's such a pain.

Emily's room is pretty nice, even if it isn't exactly my taste. She has the same pale blue carpet that I do, but her bed has a beautiful white lacy comforter and all these lace pillows all over it. The best part of her room is the stereo with the CD player that she'd bought over the summer, and this beautiful wood vanity with a big mirror attached to it that she can sit in front of and put her makeup on and fix her hair and stuff.

I picked Pepper up from Emily's bed and took her out of the room without saying a word. Emily was busy reading something and she didn't even look up.

That's when I heard Mom's keys in the door. I hadn't realized how late it was. I decided it might be better in the long run if I told her about flag now, so that on top of everything else, at least she couldn't be mad that I'd waited to tell her. So I went down the stairs very slowly, trying to figure out what I was going to say.

Mom was sitting at the kitchen table. She looked exhausted. I hated to bother her, so I turned around very quietly and tried to get out the door without being seen, but it didn't work.

"Hi, Katie. How was your day?" Mom asked as she got up and went over to the refrigerator.

"Okay, I guess," I said. "How was yours?"

"Exhausting!" Mom said in her grumpy voice. "How was the lasagna?"

"Great, Mom. Thanks for making it," I said.

She helped herself to some and sat back down at the table.

"Katie, what is the ice cream doing on the counter? How could you leave a mess like that?"

"Sorry," I mumbled. I figured this was not the time to tell her about quitting the flag squad.

"Oh, hi, Mom!" Emily said as she came bouncing into the kitchen in her bathrobe and slippers. She took a glass out of the cabinet. "So, Katie," she said in this sweet voice as though suddenly we were best friends, "I hear Central's junior high football team is undefeated. Aren't you guys playing them this weekend? Everyone must be really psyched. Did you learn any new routines for the game?"

I just glared at her. Leave it to Princess

Emily to bring up the absolutely worst topic of conversation imaginable. Now I had to tell them. I'd be lying if I didn't.

"I guess so," I finally replied.

They both just looked at me.

"What do you mean, you guess so?" Emily asked. "Did you or didn't you?"

That was more like the Emily I know and love.

"You see," I began. I took a deep breath. "I quit the flag squad today."

Emily's mouth dropped open. She looked as shocked as if I'd said I was going to the moon or something. "You what?" she finally sputtered.

My mother looked kind of upset, too. She didn't say anything at all for a few minutes. She just pursed her lips together in this really tight line and stared at me. Mom thinks being a flag girl will help me later in life. The only thing I can see it teaching me is how to yell loudly and wave a flag around.

"Well, why did you do it?" Emily asked as she sat down at the table with us, the surprised expression still on her face.

"Yes," Mom agreed, "I'd like to know why."

"Well," I began. I didn't know what to say. I didn't want to lie, but I didn't want to tell the whole truth either. "I...um...I just don't want to do it anymore."

"That's your answer?" Mom asked with a frown. She was looking at me really closely, almost as if she was examining me. I was waiting for her to feel my forehead to check if I had a fever. I had never disobeyed her or intentionally done anything that I knew she wouldn't like before.

I nodded my head yes.

"Well, I wish you'd think about this some more," Mom said.

"But, Mom —" I began.

"Katie, it's for your own good. Anyway, you should never have quit the squad without discussing it with me in the first place."

I looked at Emily, but she had a blank expression on her face. Somehow I knew I wasn't going to be a flag girl again, though.

"Mom," I said, "I don't need to think about it. I don't want to be a flag girl."

Mom and Emily looked really surprised.

Then Mom just got up from the table and walked out of the kitchen. Emily gave me what

I call her "big sister" smile. I know she means well and everything, but I could tell what was coming — sisterly advice.

"Katie," Emily said gently, "you just have to be patient with flag. It'll be great, wait and see. Anyway, it'll break Mom's heart if you quit."

That was all I needed to hear. I just couldn't understand how my being miserable was going to make Mom happy. I jumped up and ran to my room.

Chapter Four

The week passed in a sort of a blur. By Friday I felt a little better. As much as I hated having to tell my mother, I was glad that I quit flag. And as far as Stacy and Eva were concerned, I just hoped they wouldn't bring up the undershirt thing in front of anyone. So far they hadn't, but just to be on the safe side, I put all my undershirts in a bag and stuffed them at the back of my closet.

I was really looking forward to the weekend. Sabs and Randy and Allison and I planned this really great sleep-over at Sabs's house Friday night. Then we planned to go to a movie at the mall Saturday afternoon. On Sunday I planned to take Randy to Elm Park and teach her to ice-skate.

The last period before lunch I had gym. I was really nervous about seeing Mrs. O'Neal after quitting flag. Fortunately, she didn't say anything to me during gym and I relaxed a little bit.

Then, fifteen minutes before the period was over, Mrs. O'Neal dismissed us early and asked to see me. I followed her into her little office with the glass door and sat down in the chair opposite her. There were newspaper clippings on the walls showing her with different sports people. There was even one of her with Wayne Gretzky, who's my all-time favorite sports star. Mrs. O'Neal runs this program for handicapped kids, and she often gets sports celebrities to be guest instructors.

Mrs. O'Neal sat down at her desk and smiled at me. "Katie," she began, "do you want to tell me what happened on Monday?" She looked sincere and as if she really cared, but I couldn't tell her that it all started with Stacy teasing me about a stupid undershirt.

"Monday?" I said. "Nothing really happened," I continued, looking down at my feet.

"Katie, if you don't want to tell me, that's okay, but I hope you'll reconsider joining the squad," Mrs. O'Neal said with a smile. "You're one of our best flag girls."

What was it about the flag squad? Why did

everyone think it was such a big deal?

"Thank you," I replied quietly. "But I don't think I want to be on the squad right now."

I smiled shyly at her, said thank you again, and hurried back to the locker room. It was empty. The bell for next period rang just as I was in the middle of changing out of my gym clothes. Luckily, I was only going to lunch.

When I got to the cafeteria, Sabrina, Allison, and Randy were at a table toward the back of the room. I noticed that Scottie Silver was sitting at a table right next to them. I whizzed through the lunch line. I had to take a seat in the only spot left, which happened to face Scottie's table. I shot Sabs an "I'm going to get you for this" look. I knew she picked that table on purpose.

Anyway, he was sitting with his usual gang of eighth-grade jocks — Brian Williams, Flip Walsh, Joe Prescott, and Peter Mullens. They were all dressed in the same jeans, plaid flannel shirts, and varsity letter jackets. Those guys never took off those jackets, even when they were inside. They were their trademark.

"So," Randy said, popping the top off her yogurt, "what did O'Neal want?"

I took my cheese sandwich out of the brown paper bag, relieved that I hadn't brought peanut butter and jelly. What if Scottie had seen me eating baby food!

"Oh," I answered, trying to sound casual, "nothing really."

Randy shrugged and licked her spoon. As I said, she knows when to bug you and when not to.

"Well," Sabs began, "can you guys believe that it's already the end of October? It's time for the famous hockey tryouts. Who do you think is going to make the team?"

I guess Brian Williams heard her, because he turned around. "Did someone mention the hockey team?" he asked. "You've got the whole team right here — everybody who matters, anyway." All the guys started laughing.

"Wait a second," said Scottie. "You mean the whole team is sitting right here, in my seat. I'm the only one who can play the game."

The rest of the guys started booing him and throwing food in his direction. He put his hands up to his face to avoid getting hit, and started to throw some food back.

Randy slowly put down her yogurt. "You

bingo heads make me sick," she said. "You're just a bunch of dumb jocks."

"What did you call us?" Brian asked. He had turned really red.

Randy laughed. "You wouldn't understand it if I said it again, anyway, so I won't waste my breath. I just wouldn't be so sure that nobody can beat you, if I were you," she finished, sounding really mysterious.

"What are you talking about?" Scottie asked angrily, his blue eyes flashing. "I'm the best skater in the county. Ask anybody. They'll tell ya. And anyway —" he stopped and pointed at her —"who do you know that can beat me or any of us?"

Randy just kept smiling. "I know somebody who's a better skater than you," she announced loudly.

"Yeah," said Scottie, "I repeat, who is he?"

"It's not a *he*," Randy replied heatedly. "It's a *she*. That's right, a girl," said Randy when Scottie looked surprised. "And she happens to be sitting right here."

I looked around our table. Sabs could barely skate, and Allison is really slow. And then it hit me. Randy couldn't possibly mean...

"Katie. Katie Campbell," Randy announced.

"You've got to be kidding," Scottie said. "No girl, I don't care how good she is, can out-skate me."

"You make me sick," said Randy. "You're just so scared that a girl could be better than you that you're trying to sound tough in front of all your friends."

"Look, I'm the best in Acorn Falls," Scottie yelled, pushing a lock of blond hair out of his eyes. "And don't you forget it."

All the guys at his table cheered.

I was in shock. I kept wondering why the bell didn't ring or something.

"Ha!" Randy yelled back. "We'll see about that next week when Katie tries out for the hockey team!"

A hush fell over the cafeteria, and all eyes, including Scottie's, were on me.

Chapter Five

It seemed like a year before the bell rang and the cafeteria started to clear out. Lots of kids were staring at me and whispering on their way out. I was still in shock. I wanted to crawl under the table.

"Can you believe him, talking about girls like that?" Randy said as she gathered up her books. "Well, at least Mr. Big Mouth finally shut up."

"You're calling *him* Mr. Big Mouth?" I said, finding my voice at last. "What about you? How could you do this to me?"

"Katie," Randy said, her hoop earrings shaking all over the place as she leaned toward me, "don't you get it? I did it for you. You can't let him get away with saying stuff like that."

All I knew was that Randy had just told the whole school I would be trying out for the boys' ice hockey team next week. I felt sick. I picked up my backpack and walked toward the door.

"Katie," Sabs called, "where are you going?"

"I have to go to class," I yelled over my shoulder.

I spent the rest of the afternoon trying to avoid everybody. I kept getting stares from all the other kids, but honestly, I was so upset, they didn't even bother me. How could I try out for the boys' hockey team? That's just it — it's the *boys'* hockey team.

When the final bell rang, I jumped out of my seat and ran to my locker. When I got there, Sabs had left a note saying she and Allison were going on ahead to get things ready for the sleep-over.

Great. That meant I'd have to walk over with Randy, and I just didn't want to talk to her right now. I was hoping to have some time with Sabs first, so I wouldn't be so mad at Randy. I considered skipping the sleep-over and going right home, but then I'd end up telling my mom or Emily what happened. So Sabs's house was it.

I walked out the front door, and there was

Randy leaning against the brick wall, looking bored. I tried to walk past her, hoping she wouldn't see me, but no such luck.

"Hey, Katie, wait up!" Randy called out.

I turned around. "Oh, hi," I said, trying to sound normal. "I guess you're on your way over to Sabs's."

"Yeah," said Randy, "I thought we could walk over together."

"Listen," she began after we had walked a little distance away from school, "about this afternoon, in the cafeteria, remember?"

I frowned. "How could I forget?"

"Well, I'm sorry I got so carried away. But I meant what I said. You can't let Scottie and those guys get away with saying girls aren't as good as boys."

"You mean *you* can't let guys get away with saying it!" I said, getting kind of upset. "Why did you have to bring me into it? What am I going to do now?"

We took the shortcut to Sabrina's house. The tree-lined streets looked so beautiful in their blankets of red and gold leaves. I blew a puff of steam out of my mouth. It was definitely getting closer to winter. I always measure how cold it really is by how much steam I can see coming out of my mouth.

"I heard you quit the flag squad," Randy said, changing the subject.

"Yeah," I replied. "I quit."

"So," she said slowly, "I guess you finally had it with cheering on those self-centered boys. Don't you think it's time girls had a chance to prove they're just as good?"

I had to admit she had a point. That's so Randy. You could bet that if she could skate, she would be trying out for the boys' hockey team, just because it was something no girl here had ever done.

The more I thought about it, even though I was absolutely terrified, the more excited I got. I had definitely, without a doubt, lost my mind.

We got to Sabrina's street, and Randy turned around to face me.

"Look, I just think that if you're good, you ought to show the world. You can't be stopped by anybody, certainly not by a bunch of guys."

"Well, I'll think about it," I said to her with a smile. I really wasn't angry anymore. She had apologized, and anyway, I knew that she believed that she'd really done it for me.

"Yup," she said, and she had this big grin on her face. "Just think about it. Hey, it's freezing. Let's get to Sabrina's!"

I love going to Sabs's house. It's really big and old, and what with four brothers, her parents, and all their pets, the house is usually a madhouse. I mean, there's always something going on there. Sabs complains that she doesn't have any privacy and she hardly ever gets to use the phone, but I think her home is really cool.

I called Mom when I got there to let her know everything was okay. When I got off the phone, Sam and his two best friends, Nick Robbins and Jason McKee, had come in. Everyone was starved, so we ordered three big pizzas with everything. Well, actually, it was three big pizzas with three different combinations. When the pizzas arrived, we all sat around the Wellses' huge kitchen table and ate pizza and talked.

I like Nick and Jason a lot. I didn't know them well back in the sixth grade, but since I'm best friends with Sabs this year, I've gotten to know them better. Nick went out with Stacy the Great last year, but they hardly speak to each other this year. Nick happens to be really cute. He has blond hair and blue eyes, and he's a lot of fun. Personally, I think he has a crush on Sabs. He asked her to go to the homecoming dance, but then for all these complicated reasons it didn't work out the way he wanted. He did dance with Sabrina for the special spotlight dance that we planned for her. And they both looked really happy at the end.

Jason's also really cute. He has brown hair and brown eyes and he's kind of shy. I think Allison sort of likes him, but she claims boys don't interest her at all. I don't know about that. And then there's Sam. He's definitely the leader of the group. I like him a lot, as I've said before, but I don't think he's my type. I think he's more like a brother.

"So, Katie," Nick said through a mouthful of pizza, "I heard what happened during your lunch period today."

"Yeah," Sam said, "you gonna try out for the team or what?" He practically inhaled his slice of pizza in one bite.

The three of them laughed.

"Of course she's going to try out," Sabs answered for me.

Sam made a face at her. Sabs made one back.

"Come on, guys," Sabs said. "Let's go up to my room."

We climbed the two flights of steps to her room in the attic. It's a great room. It has sloped walls and it's really cozy. Sabs proceeded to tell us all about her latest crush on Michael Winston, a boy from our math class.

"Michael Winston!" I exclaimed. "He looks like a rabbit, his teeth stick out so much. And he has those really thick glasses."

"Sabs, you have a new crush every week!" said Allison. "Even I'm having trouble keeping it all straight."

Allison was sitting in this really cool rocking chair that Sabrina has, and Randy was lying on her bed. I was sitting in front of Sabs because she was trying to French-braid my hair. As soon as I said that about Michael Winston, she pulled my hair so tight, my head hurt.

"Hey, be careful!" I said.

"You take that back about Michael," Sabs replied, loosening her grip. "And, Allison, if you value your friend Katie, you'll take back what you said, too!"

"What did I say, Sabs?" asked Allison innocently.

Randy giggled. "I don't have a clue about who you're talking about. I'm sure it's not that guy with the really thick glasses!"

With that, we all collapsed into hysterical giggles.

A little while later we changed into our pajamas and got comfortable. Randy had put on the biggest T-shirt I had ever seen in my life. It had these really neat people drawn all over it. I had my flannel nightgown and matching slippers that my mother bought me especially for sleep-overs. At first I felt kind of weird putting them on because I thought someone was going to make a mean comment. But everyone loved them and asked where my mother got the set. Even Randy asked. She said she'd probably need something like that with the harsh winters here and all.

Then Sabs brought out this game that she wanted us to play. Sabs said her mother bought it after they discussed the sleep-over. It was a pretty fun game. If you got wrong answers, you had to put these plastic zits on your face. At first Randy didn't want to play, but she did anyway and had to put three zits on her face for wrong answers. Sabrina took pictures of all of us with these red zits on our faces. What a hoot.

By the time I crawled into my sleeping bag on Sabrina's floor, I felt all was right with the world again. And I knew I had the coolest friends in the whole world.

Chapter Six

On Saturday morning we had this incredible breakfast with the Wells family. I mean, there must have been a thousand people in their kitchen. Actually, there were only ten of us, it just felt like a thousand, since I'm just used to Mom and Emily and me at breakfast.

We had decided to get to the mall around eleven o'clock so that we'd have time to go into stores and stuff before the movie started. Of course, the minute we touched foot into the mall, Sabs wanted to go to Dare, her absolute favorite store of all time. I was in the mood to go exploring alone, so I went into this store called The Ultimate. I told everyone I'd meet them at the movie.

The store was pretty crowded and the music was really loud. The sale rack was in the back. It was one of those long ones, on wheels, and since it's always packed with stuff, you kind of have to stand behind it to look at any of the clothes. I was standing there, behind the rack where nobody could see me, when I heard Eva Malone's voice. She must have been standing in front of the rack.

"She what?" she practically screamed.

She was talking really loudly, so that I could hear her over the noise of all the other kids and the music.

"You're kidding me," she continued. "I don't believe it."

"Well, believe it," another voice said. "I was there." That was B.Z. She wasn't talking as loudly, but I was straining my ears to hear.

"Randy Zak told Scottie Silver off at lunch on Friday," B.Z. went on. "She told him he was scared that a girl could be better him. And then she said Katie Campbell was going to try out for the boys' ice hockey team on Monday. Isn't that incredible?"

I couldn't believe they were talking about me. I'm not the kind of person people talk about. It made me feel funny — kind of important, but also really nervous. I wondered how long I'd have to stand there behind the rack, waiting for them to leave. The last thing I needed was Eva starting in on me, especially in front of a store full of strangers.

"Well," said Eva. "Stacy's going out with him tonight. She'll get the whole story."

"Let's go," said B.Z. "This store is played."

I stayed behind the rack for a few more minutes to make sure they'd really gone. I didn't even want to stay in the mall, since I was afraid I'd bump into Eva or B.Z. But I couldn't stay behind the sale rack in The Ultimate forever. Anyway, Sabs, Allison, and Randy were expecting me at the movie. I took a deep breath and peeked out from behind the clothes like I was a spy or something. The coast was clear. The store was still packed, but there wasn't any sign of Eva or B.Z. or anyone else from that group.

I took the escalator up to the movie theater. Sabs was already there, waiting in front of the place where you can get popcorn and candy and stuff.

When Randy and Allison showed up, I told them what B.Z. and Eva had said in the store.

"Don't worry about it," said Sabs, putting her arm around my shoulder. "As I always say, any guy that likes Stacy can't be right for us."

"In my school, back in New York..." Randy started.

Sabs and I looked at each other and rolled our eyes. "Back in New York" is probably Randy's favorite phrase in the entire English language.

"...you would never hear a guy say anything like Scottie had said," Randy continued. "If he did, everyone would be all over him in a second. It's up to us to show this backward town how to act."

Sabs gave Randy a look. I think she was annoyed that Randy had dared to call Acorn Falls a backward town.

"No offense, Sabs," Randy went on, noticing the look. "You know what I mean."

Sabs sort of smiled.

It's funny how different Randy is from all of us. Well, actually she's different from everyone else in Acorn Falls. I mean, she used to go to this really weird school in New York City where everybody was rich and they didn't even get grades, and she had never even heard of homecoming. She also says whatever's on her mind, even to a teacher. She even talked back to Ms. Staats, our homeroom teacher, and didn't get detention. The only other seventh-grade girl I know who's at all like that is Eva, but she just has a big mouth and says stupid things. Randy always says things that seem to make sense.

Anyway, the movie was great, but I think it made Randy a little bit homesick because it took place in New York. She looked sort of down when Sabs's father picked us up. He invited us all over for dinner, but Randy wanted to go home. I decided it was time for me to go home, too.

On Sunday I met Randy at Elm Park right after lunch. It had been so cold for the past week that the pond there had finally frozen over. Randy had definitely dressed for the occasion. She was wearing neon-orange tights, a red miniskirt with an electric-blue sweater, and a bright yellow hat. She looked kind of like a box of crayons. Her mother had given her these ancient figure skates that were hers twenty years ago, but the blades looked okay, so I told her I thought she'd be fine.

We laced up our skates and she hobbled out onto the ice. There weren't a lot of people, so we had the place to ourselves. That was a good thing, since it didn't seem as if Randy wanted an audience. Usually she loves calling attention to herself, but today she was being really quiet. I guess she was nervous. I wondered how many people had ever seen her quiet like this.

I explained the basics of skating to Randy very carefully. I explained to her how important it is to keep the ankles straight and lean forward. Then I grabbed her hand, and the two of us started to skate. At least, I did, but then Randy caught her toe pick in the ice and went flying. Of course, I went flying, too, since I was holding her hand.

I had to struggle to keep myself from laughing, but Randy looked so funny sitting there on the ice, with this big frown on her face and that glow-in-the-dark hat. I helped her up, and then we tried again.

This time she did a little better, but she still seemed really uncomfortable on her ice skates. I guess maybe learning to skate when you're really young, like I did, is easier than trying to learn when you're older. I mean, I know Randy's really coordinated. She's a whiz on her skateboard.

"Katie," Randy suddenly said, "why don't you skate for a while, and I'll practice by myself." I could tell she was getting really frustrated.

"Are you sure you'll be okay?" I asked.

"Of course," Randy replied and tossed her head so that her hat fell off.

We both reached to grab it and managed to knock our heads together by mistake and to fall down once again. This time I couldn't help it. I laughed. Then I looked over at Randy. She was laughing, too.

"Let's try skating backward," Randy suggested. "I have this weird feeling that it will be easier for me."

Of course, Randy was right. Anyway, we stayed at Elm Park until right before dinner. Randy actually got the hang of skating backward. Of course, we used the "hourglass" method, and she couldn't go very fast like that, but she seemed to really like the fact that she was skating backward. We made plans to have another skating lesson next weekend. I still couldn't believe that Randy wanted to learn how to skate. She was really full of surprises.

Chapter Seven

For some reason, whenever I have to do something I don't want to do after school, the day passes really quickly. Well, that's what happened on Monday. Even the pop quiz in social studies was a breeze compared to what I was expecting at hockey tryouts.

Sabs, Randy, Allison, and I had planned to meet at the front entrance of school and walk over to the rink together. Sabs had brought me a pair of her brother Mark's old hockey skates, so I was ready in that department. I had also decided that morning that it was time for me to wear a bra. And that now would be a great time for me to get used to wearing one, because I didn't have to worry about anybody seeing me while I was changing. So that morning I put on one of Emily's old bras. Boy! I wish I had thought it through. It turned out to be a disaster!

"Your horoscope says that something is going to happen to change your life very soon," Sabs informed me as we neared the rink.

"I'm sure she's thrilled to death, Sabs," Randy said.

I didn't say anything. I was in a daze.

"I think it means something good is going to happen," Sabs said indignantly.

I don't believe in horoscopes, but I was happy for any help I could get. By then we were at the rink and I had to keep myself from turning around and running out. Randy opened the door and practically had to push me inside.

"Don't look now," Sabs whispered to me. "But Stacy the Great and her clones are here." She nodded her head in their direction.

I sat down on a low bleacher, took my jacket off, and took a deep breath. Sabs is always telling me that's what you're supposed to do to calm down. I could feel a lot of eyes on me, and I squirmed uncomfortably. I'd never gotten so much attention in my life. It definitely felt weird.

"What are you guys staring at?" Randy asked. "Haven't you ever seen a girl before?"

I guess that caught Brian Williams's attention, because he looked up and elbowed Scottie in the side. Scottie just glanced at me for a second, shrugged at Brian as if he could care less, and skated away.

The coach blew his whistle and all of us had to go out onto the main arena. His name is Coach Budd, and he's got this big beer belly and a very red face. He's been coaching hockey for ages, and he's known for being tough. Somebody once said that a long time ago he played for the Minnesota North Stars. One of the players was handing out tryout numbers, and when he got to me he called Coach Budd over.

"What's going on here?" the coach asked, annoyed.

"I want to try out for the team," I replied really softly.

"You what?" he said, putting his hands on his hips.

Everybody at the entire rink was watching us. I was practically shaking.

"Look, what's your name?" he asked me.

"Katie. Katie Campbell," I said in this trembly voice.

"Look, Katie," Coach Budd said more nicely, "I'm trying to conduct a tryout here. You can come for the free skating session tomorrow. The rink will be open to everyone then."

"No, you don't understand," I said, still softly but more firmly. "I mean...I...well...I want to try out for the hockey team."

I could hear all the guys laughing.

"Quit it!" the coach yelled at them. "I'm sorry, Katie, but there never has been and there never will be a girl on my hockey team. It's a boys' sport and that's it."

And then the strangest thing happened. Shy and quiet Allison stood up. "I'm sorry, Coach," she said in this loud, clear voice, "but by law you are required to let Katie play."

Everybody in the rink just stared at her, including Coach Budd, who was standing there with his mouth hanging open.

I whirled around. I couldn't believe that Allison had actually spoken up and told a teacher he was wrong. Most kids would never have the guts to do that, let alone Allison.

"Don't you remember Title IX?" Allison asked. The coach didn't answer, so Allison kept on talking.

"Well, in 1972, Title IX of the Federal Education Amendment stated that 'no person in the United States shall, on the basis of sex, be excluded from participating in, be denied the benefits of, or be subjected to discrimination under any education program or activity receiving federal financial assistance.' And that includes athletic teams. So, sir," Allison continued taking a deep breath, "I guess that means you'll have to let Katie try out for the team, or you'll be breaking the law."

Then she sat down. Randy started clapping, and so did Sabs. But the coach gave them such a mean look, they stopped.

Then the coach told the kid who was handing out the numbers to give me one. Without looking at me, he told me to go suit up. I couldn't believe I was actually doing it.

I followed some of the other guys, picked up a uniform, and started walking into the locker room when somebody tapped me on the shoulder. I turned around. It was Scottie, and he didn't look very friendly.

"You can't go in there," Scottie said. "It's the boys' locker room, see?" he continued, pointing to the sign.

I started to blush. I was really embarrassed.

"I knew that," I said, trying to act tough. Actually, I didn't even know if there was a girls' locker room, and even if there was, I had no idea where.

I walked out and started looking around. I felt like an idiot just standing there. I wanted to cry. But then Flip came up to me. "If you're looking for a place to change," he said with a grin, "the visitors' locker room is over there." He pointed to the other side of the rink.

I gave him a big smile and turned to go.

"Katie," Flip called.

I turned. "Yeah?" I said.

"Good luck," he replied and smiled back at me.

"Thanks, I'll need it," I replied.

I hurried to the visitors' locker room, but when I got there, all the lights were off. I groped around, looking for the switch, but I couldn't find it anywhere. I heard the coach blow the whistle and yell out a two-minute warning. I'd just have to get dressed in the dark.

It was sort of creepy being all alone in this room in the dark. There was one window in the back that let in some light, so at least I was able to see a little bit. I pulled my shirt off, and then I remembered that I was wearing Emily's bra. It was definitely too big and it was sort of bunching up on the sides. I wasn't sure if I should take it off or not, but it was kind of uncomfortable and it had been riding up my back all day. I sure didn't want to be out there on the ice in front of all those guys, pulling my bra down. I decided to take it off. I tried to unhook it, but it just wouldn't work. I was twisting all over the place with my hands behind my back. Finally I just pulled the straps off my shoulders, got my arms out, and turned the bra around so the hook was facing me. I unhooked it and pulled it off.

By that time my heart was beating like crazy. I could hear a lot of cheering and noise outside in the arena, and I knew I was late. I quickly pulled my jeans off and got into the rest of my uniform. Luckily, I knew how to put on the uniform from watching my dad so many times before. There were these shoulder pads, shin guards, elbow pads, and hip and thigh pads. I felt like a mattress. Then I sat down on the bench and laced up my skates.

The coach had already divided everyone up into groups by the time I got out on the ice. I tried to ignore all of the stares and snickers from the kids watching in the bleachers and all of the dirty looks from the guys on the team. I heard Randy, Allison, and Sabs yelling, "Way to go, Katie!" which sort of embarrassed me, but also made me feel a little better.

I really wanted to turn around and wave to Sabs, Al, and Randy, but I figured that would be totally uncool. I looked around at the guys, and they were all either looking at the games being played on the ice or talking to one another.

"Okay," Coach Budd finally said, rubbing his hands together. "Let's get out there and get to work."

Suddenly the coach blew his whistle. Everybody stopped what they were doing.

"Campbell, what's with your uniform?" Coach Budd yelled.

"Hey, look behind you, Katie," Scottie said as he skated over to me.

Everybody in the arena laughed. I pulled my shirt around and there was that stupid bra hanging down my pants!

If I thought I was ever embarrassed before, now I knew that I had really lost it. I could feel everyone's eyes on me. Of course, they knew it wasn't my bra. Everybody could see that I was flat-chested and sure didn't need one. Now, what was I supposed to do with it?

"Katie, please finish dressing in the visitors' changing room," said Coach Budd. He surprised me: he didn't sound mad or anything. I rolled the bra up in my hand and skated to the changing room. I shoved the bra into my bag and sat down on the bench with a thud.

Boy! I've really blown it now, I thought.

I looked up and there were Allison, Randy, and Sabrina.

"How did the bra get stuck there, Katie?" Sabrina asked right away.

"I don't know!" I screamed, and started to cry. "I guess I was rushing to get into my uniform and it got caught on the back of my pants. I'm not sure! What am I going to do? How can I go back out there?" I cried.

"I guess you'll just have to skate back out there," said Allison softly.

Suddenly I heard the coach's whistle.

"Campbell!" he called. "Get out here!"

I skated back out on the ice. Everybody started laughing again.

"Knock it off!" the coach yelled again. "This is not a joke, it's a tryout. Now everybody just settle down and get back to work."

Everyone lined up to go Indian Skating. We lined up in single file around the rink. The last person in line had to sprint up to the front and then continue moving around the rink. Then, the new last person had to do the same thing all over again. We did that drill until everybody had a chance at being first, including me. Then we did a few other drills. They were really hard, but at least it got me to stop thinking about the bra. I wondered if I'd ever live it down.

Finally we were finished. I skated off the ice, took my helmet off, and sat down for a second to catch my breath. Most of the other guys were doing the same thing so I figured it was okay.

"I saw a lot of good skating out here today," Coach Budd began. "Keep up the good work, and we'll have a winning team. I'll see you all tomorrow."

I got up and started back to the locker room. Randy, Sabs, and Allison came flying out of the bleachers and ran up to me. I stopped walking and waited for them.

"Katie," Sabs gushed, "you were incredible out there! You were the best one! I bet you'll make the team for sure!"

"How could you tell?" I asked her. "We just did a bunch of drills."

"I thought you were really good, too," Allison said quietly.

"Thanks, Allison," I replied, "but there were a lot of guys out there who are much better than me. Anyway, I just hope I don't die before this whole thing is over. I'm exhausted."

"Well," Sabs said, "we're thinking of going to Fitzie's. You're coming, right? And don't worry about the bra thing."

"Sabrina," Randy said, elbowing her.

"Okay," I said. "Let's go. But you may have to carry me there." I sighed and rubbed my arm. I felt muscles hurt that I didn't even know I had. "Let me get dressed, and I'll meet you in here in a couple of minutes."

I took a really quick shower, being really careful not to get my hair wet, since I'd forgotten to bring my blow dryer, and then I started to get dressed. This time I made sure the bra was in my bag.

When we got to Fitzie's we all stopped in the doorway and surveyed the room. I noticed that Scottie, Brian, Flip, and some other guys from the hockey team were over in the far left corner near the jukebox. Stacy, Eva, Laurel, and B.Z. were hanging out there, too. They were all sharing French fries, and they looked like they were having a great time, laughing and everything. Whoever sits at that table gets to control the jukebox. Naturally, every year only the most popular kids get that table. This year Scottie and his group sat there.

The only empty booth was a few tables away from Scottie and those guys in the back. Sabrina and everyone ran to the table. I walked straight to the table without looking at anybody.

"What'll it be?" a waitress in a red-and-white-checked uniform asked us.

"Diet Coke over here," Randy said. Randy always has diet food, as if she isn't skinny enough already.

"Wanna split an ice cream soda, Al?" Sabs practically pleaded. I knew Sabs would drink the whole thing. Allison almost never eats sweets.

Allison smiled and said, "Okay."

The waitress looked at me. "Nothing, thanks," I said. I was too pooped to eat.

Sabs took the paper off her straw and stuck it in her mouth. She turned around to see what was happening behind her.

I guess Stacy could feel us staring at her because she turned around and caught my gaze. "Well, well," Stacy proclaimed in a really loud voice, "if it isn't Katie Campbell, the ice-hockey queen."

Everybody at her table and every other table within hearing distance looked at me. Unfortunately, I was trapped in the booth. Randy was sitting firmly next to me, and she wasn't budging to let me out. She would never walk away from these confrontations. I just wanted to crawl under the table.

"So, Katie," Eva continued loudly, "maybe you need lessons on how to wear a bra!"

She and Stacy and some other kids started to laugh.

"Good one, Eva," Brian said, hitting the table.

"I wouldn't talk, Eva," Randy said. "No guy

would ever notice if you wore a bra or not — I mean, with your attitude."

Somebody tittered.

"Shut up, Zak!" Stacy cut in.

"Hey, Katie," Scottie suddenly said, "you better watch out from now on. Those guys were just being nice today. Wait till we start playing tough."

Stacy and Eva looked smugly at me.

"Look," I said, motioning for Randy to let me out, "I'm really tired. I'm going home."

Sabs got up, too. "I'll walk with you," she said.

The two of us made a beeline for the door with our heads together, pretending we were deep in conversation so nobody could bother us. The last thing I heard before I escaped out the door was, "Just wait, she'll get what she deserves."

Chapter Eight

"Katie, is that you?" Emily called out as soon as I walked in the door.

I considered turning around and running, but Emily had flown down the stairs and seen me before I could make my getaway.

"I want to talk to you," Emily said gravely. She folded her arms in front of her chest. I turned and walked into the kitchen, with her one step behind me. "When Mom finds out that you've joined the hockey team, she's going to be really mad."

I took the milk out of the refrigerator and poured myself a glass. "Where is Mom, any-way?" I asked, trying not to sound too interest-ed. Actually, Emily was right. Mom was going to be fuming, especially after what happened last week. I just hoped that she wasn't adding up all the things that I'd done wrong lately. If she did that, I probably wouldn't be allowed out of the house until I was seventy years old.

"She called about ten minutes ago," Emily informed me. "She's working late at the office, which, I might add," she continued, "is very lucky for you.

"Katie," Emily said changing to her 'older sister' voice, "it's very daring of you to have tried out for the team, but girls don't play ice hockey."

I looked at her without saying anything.

"Look, Katie," Emily continued in the same voice, "Mom and I just want you to be happy. I mean, people are already talking about you, and they're not saying the most flattering things."

"So tell them I'm not really your sister," I said. "Say you found me wandering in the jungle when I was two years old and adopted me. How's that?"

"Why are you being so hostile?" Emily said. "I'm just trying to help."

I took my glass of milk and went into the living room. I saw the headlights through the living room window. Mom. It wouldn't be long now. The car door closed, and I could hear Mom walking up the front path. Emily ran to the door and opened it.

"Hi, girls," Mom said when she walked in. She went into the living room and sat down on the couch. Emily and I followed her.

I think our living room is really beautiful. It looks like it's out of a magazine. There are vases filled with cut flowers on all the tables. The couch is cream-colored with dusty-rose throw pillows, and sits in front of two long windows that face the front of the house. Mom's really big on cream and dusty rose. There's a piano in one corner with framed pictures on top of it. There's a picture of Emily and me when we were little, holding up this huge fish we'd caught. Then there's one of those school pictures of me that was taken last year, and one of Emily in her pom-pom uniform. Mom took down all the ones of Dad after he died. I guess they made her too sad.

There are two chairs facing the couch. They're both cream-colored, with dusty-rose stripes. I decided to sit on one of them. Emily sat down on the couch next to Mom. I felt like it was two against one. It just wasn't fair.

"Katie, please come and sit down beside me," Mom began. "I just received some rather upsetting news. I ran into Mrs. Simons in the supermarket and she told me that Hilary told her that you had tried out for the boys' ice hockey team." Then she just stared at me for a minute without saying anything else. I could feel Emily's eyes on me, too. She was shooting me sympathy looks, but a fat lot of good they were going to do me now. Mom was really, really mad.

"Didn't we have a discussion about this last week, Katherine?" Mom finally asked. She said each word very slowly and quietly. I knew it was bad. She only called me Katherine when she was really mad.

I didn't say anything, since I could tell she wasn't really asking me a question.

"Yes, you did," Emily cut in, giving me a look and acting as if she was doing me a big favor by answering for me.

Mom looked sideways at Emily. "I remember what I said." She turned to me. "I told you I didn't want you playing rough with the boys," Mom said, looking at me very hard.

"Yes, you did, but —"

"Look," Mom interrupted me. She wasn't interested in anything I had to say to defend myself. "I don't want to hear anything more about ice hockey. You will not try out for the team, Katherine. Do I make myself clear?"

I didn't say anything. Mom must have taken that to mean I would do what she wanted, because she got up. I couldn't just let her do that to me. I mean, as much as I hated to get into trouble, I just had to go through with the rest of the tryouts. I couldn't let my mother and Emily run my whole life for me.

"Mom, can I please just explain what happened?" I pleaded.

"There is nothing to explain," she said. "I don't want to discuss it anymore."

Discuss it? I didn't think we'd had a discussion. Mom had done all of the talking. I started to get really angry. She hadn't even let me explain. I have always been a very calm person, but this was different. I knew I deserved a chance. Before I could stop myself, I got up out of my chair and turned squarely toward Mom. I felt like a different person. I was practically shaking.

"I'm going to try out for the hockey team," I said, my voice rising, "whether you want me to or not. I don't want to be a flag girl just because

Emily was a flag girl. I want to play hockey like Dad. He would have let me. He would have wanted me to do it!"

Tears were streaming down my face. Mom's mouth was hanging open in shock. I was shocked, too. I had never talked back to her or even raised my voice before. But this time was different. I wanted to try out for the team, and she didn't have one good reason not to let me.

I ran out of the living room and up to my bedroom. I slammed the door. A few minutes later I heard knocking. I lay really still, trying to pretend I was asleep.

"Katie," Mom said softly as she opened the door. "Katie, I'd like to talk to you."

"Mmmmm," I muttered into my pillows.

"Katie," Mom began gently, "you know how much I hate to see you upset, but you have to understand that I'm only trying to do what's best for you. And that's not easy — especially without your father."

I flipped over onto my back and squinted at her in the darkness.

"You should have at least told me what you were planning to do," Mom continued. "Hearing it from Mrs. Simons was quite a shock, especially since I had to act as if I already knew."

"Sorry about that, Mom," I muttered.

"Well, you know how I feel," she finished with a sigh. "So sleep on it."

With that, Mom smoothed the hair off my face and tiptoed out of the room.

I flipped back onto my stomach. How had things gotten so complicated?

Chapter Nine

I went through school the next day a nervous wreck. When Ms. Staats, the English teacher, asked me who wrote *The Great Gatsby*, I said F. Scottie Fitzgerald. The whole class cracked up. I thought I would die. I was getting so desperate for something good to happen that I even considered talking to Sabs and consulting my horoscope to see if tomorrow would bring me better luck.

I met Sabs, Allison, and Randy at the front door after the final bell. I grabbed Mark's old skates, and the three of us walked over to the arena. Sabs hadn't heard anything from her brother Mark about what the boys were planning for me, so I tried to convince myself that nothing was going to happen and that everything would be fine. I hoped I was right.

Tuesday's tryouts were pretty much the same as Monday's, except this time I knew where to change. I picked up pads and a uniform from a table by the ice and went straight to the visitors' locker room. This time it didn't take me as long to get dressed, because someone had turned the light on for me, plus I wasn't wearing that bra.

On Wednesday, I felt as if somebody had put a load of sand into my stomach. I couldn't believe I was actually going through with this, knowing that I could be mutilated at any moment. Allison, Randy, and Sabs walked over to the arena again. Randy winked at me. "Hang tough, Katie," she said.

The coach put me in a scrimmage group with Flip. He looked a little upset when he heard Coach call my name with his. I tried to catch his eye, but he wouldn't even look at me. I knew that was bad news.

After we did some stretches and a few of the same drills we'd done the two days before, the coach blew the whistle and the first scrimmage teams had to go out onto the ice. Flip came up next to me. "Watch your back, Katie," he whispered before he skated away. Great. The guys obviously meant business.

To make matters worse, Scottie Silver was

on the other scrimmage team. On the last day of tryouts, the coach mixes the guys who are already on the team with the guys trying out to see how everybody plays together and how everybody does. Coach made me a left wing. Naturally, the center on the other team was Scottie. I could see why the coach put me at left wing. No one really wanted to play on the left side, unless he was left-handed. It's much harder to hit the puck toward the goal from the left side than the right. Brian Williams was the left wing from last year's team. He's great.

We began with the face-off. My team got the puck and the center passed it to me. But before I could move, one of the defensivemen came at me with a hip check. He hit me so hard that I rolled over him, right onto the ice.

When I got the puck the next time, Scottie boarded me and I hit the wall hard and then I hit the ice. I felt like I was being hit from both sides, and I could hardly get up. The coach didn't even call a penalty.

It seemed as if every time I stood up, one of the other players would run me down. When I finally made it into the offensive zone, dribbling the puck, the guys from my team weren't even there to pass the puck to. Then Scottie charged me, elbowed me, and tripped me. I waited for the whistle, but the coach didn't blow it.

I couldn't believe the coach was letting these guys do this to me. I mean, he had to be able to see that they were ganging up on me and everything, but he was just standing there, watching. And then it hit me. I guess he figured if that was what it took to get me off the team, he'd let them do it. He was letting them try and scare me off. Either that, or he was going to let them hurt me so badly that I'd never be able to walk again. Whichever one it was, he was determined to get rid of me, no matter what. I wasn't going to let him get away with it, though. I had never felt so determined in my life. I kept bringing the puck down the ice, and when no one ever came to help out, I just took shots on goal.

When time was up, and he finally blew the whistle, I could hardly move. I barely managed to make it over to the bench to sit down. I tried to act as if I was fine so the guys wouldn't think they'd hurt me too badly, but it was really tough. I could hardly sit there, I was so sore.

When the other scrimmages were over, I tried to walk to the locker room as normally as possible.

When I got there, I tried to pull the jersey up over my head, but I could barely lift my arms. It felt like the time when we went to the beach and I got really sunburned. After a lot of twisting and turning, I was finally able to get out of the jersey, pads, and pants. My calves were sore and my left thigh felt numb. My hipbone was also really sore. I was sure it would be black and blue by morning.

I got back into my regular clothes and lugged all of the stuff out of the locker room. When I got back to the rink, all of the guys were sitting on the bleachers, listening to the coach. I noticed that all the spectators were gone — including Randy, Al, and Sabs. He must have told them they couldn't stay. So I'd have to walk home without them. I'd been counting on them to carry my stuff for me. Oh, well. What was a little more pain?

The coach gave us a lecture about how we were all really good, and how he was so pleased that so many guys had shown up to try out. He explained that only some of us could make the team, but that didn't mean the rest of us weren't good. After what happened during the scrimmages today, I was sure I'd never make the team. And anyway, they obviously didn't want me, so none of what he was saying had anything to do with me.

When he was finished, I started to get my things together. But they were really heavy, and it took me a while to get outside. By the time I made it, most of the guys had gone.

I dropped all of my stuff on the front steps and sighed. I didn't know how I was going to make it home with all of this stuff, and I was so sore it hurt to move.

"If you're planning to play a man's game, you'd better stop acting like a wimp," somebody suddenly said.

I looked up. It was Scottie.

I'd just about had it with him and the whole hockey team. At that moment I didn't care what he thought about me at all. I was so tired, I just wanted to get home.

"Talk about wimps," I said, looking him right in the eye. "You were so scared I'd show you up out there, you had to beat me up to prove how tough you are. Well, you're not." I was really mad. I couldn't stop myself. Anyway, he deserved it. "You can't stop me, no matter what. Randy was right. You just can't stand the idea that a girl could be faster than you. Well, you'd better get used to it."

I expected him to say something really obnoxious back, but he didn't. He just stood there, looking at me. I guess I'd shocked him by talking back like that.

And then the weirdest thing happened. We were just standing there, looking at each other, when he leaned toward me and kinda brushed my cheek with his lips. Then his ride showed up and he ran down the steps real fast and got into the car.

I didn't move for a while. I couldn't believe what had just happened. One minute Scottie was telling me I was a wimp, and the next he was kissing me. Well, I think he kissed me. It happened so fast, it was hard to believe it had really happened at all.

When I was finally able to move my legs, I picked up my stuff and started walking home. I'd forgotten about all of the pain I was in, and the hockey equipment didn't even seem that heavy anymore.

I kept playing the scene over and over again in my mind. Had Scottie kissed me or not? He was either obnoxious to me or ignored me in school, and then he practically tried to kill me out on the ice. Somebody who liked you enough to kiss you wouldn't act like that. The only other thing I could come up with was that it was a joke. But that didn't make sense. I touched my cheek where he'd kissed me. I felt like never washing my face again. Boy, was I getting carried away or what? I was beginning to sound like Sabs.

When I got home, I went straight up to my room with my coat still on and dumped all of my stuff on the floor.

"Katie!" Emily yelled up the stairs.

"What do you want, Emily?" I yelled back as I opened my door. "Can't you just pick Pepper up yourself? She's had all her shots, you know."

"Just for that, I think I'll tell Sabs you're not home," Emily retorted.

"Don't you dare!" I screamed. I ran into the hall and picked up the phone. "Emily," I said into the phone. "Hang up!" I waited until I heard the click. "Hi, Sabs," I said.

"Hi," Sabs replied. "Listen, I can't believe the coach made us leave this afternoon. I mean, we really wanted to see you after tryouts and everything. Those guys were being such jerks — especially Scottie Silver."

"He's not *such* a jerk," I said.

"What?" Sabs screamed into the phone. "How can you say that after what he did to you today?"

I thought about not telling Sabs about the kiss. After all, I hadn't even figured out what it meant myself yet. And knowing Sabs, she'd make the biggest deal in the world about it. But what good was being kissed by the cutest guy in school if you're the only one who knows about it? Besides, Sabs is my best friend.

"Well, it wasn't just Scottie, you know," I said. I wanted to make her drag it out of me.

"Okay, Katie," Sabs said. "What's going on here? This afternoon he acted like the biggest jerk in the world, and now you're practically defending him."

"Nothing is going on, Sabs," I said. "It's just that…well, I guess I might as well tell you. But you've got to swear you won't tell a soul."

"Swear," she said quickly. "Now what?"

"Scottie Silver kissed me," I finally said.

"WHAT!" she screamed into the phone.

I couldn't walk, I couldn't move my arms, and now I was deaf. I hit my ear a few times with the palm of my hand. "Sabs, don't scream like that," I said. "My ears are still buzzing."

"I can't believe it," Sabs said. "I mean, Scottie Silver, junior high make-out king, kissed you! My best friend!"

"Stop, Sabs," I cut in. "It was only on the cheek, and I swear it happened so fast, I'm not even sure."

"Katie, be serious. Scottie Silver kissed you. Incredible," she gushed.

"Don't forget your promise, Sabs," I said. "You can't tell anybody."

"Yeah, yeah," she replied. "But I won't be able to sleep tonight. This is so exciting! I can't wait for school tomorrow." She laughed. "Can you imagine me saying that?"

"I'll see you tomorrow," I said. "And remember, not a word, not even to Randy or Allison, in case somebody overhears."

"I said I promised," Sabs replied. "Remember, tomorrow's a big day. It's the day they announce who made the team. Sleep well,

Katie. Bye."

We hung up. I'd practically forgotten all about the hockey team. I mean, I'd actually made it through the tryouts, basically in one piece, even though I'd probably never be able to move my arms or legs normally again. I'd also put Scottie Silver in his place, and he kind of kissed me. Try to figure seventh grade. Weird.

Chapter Ten

"Hey, let me see!" some guy said as he pushed me aside. I could see that Sabs, Randy, and Allison weren't doing any better than I was. It was Friday, and we were trying to see the list of guys who made the hockey team, but there was such a mob scene that we couldn't even get close. Kids who hadn't even tried out were trying to get a look.

"Congratulations, Katie!" somebody suddenly said. It was Kelly Lewis from the flag squad.

"She made it! She made it!" Sabs exclaimed, jumping up and down.

I almost fainted. Allison was beaming, and even Randy looked excited.

"I won't believe it until I see for myself," I said as I pushed my way to the front of the crowd. But there it was in black and white —"Katherine Campbell." It was too good to be true.

I was so excited that I couldn't stop smiling. Every time I tried to get the corners of my mouth to go down, they'd just pop up again. It was sort of embarrassing, but I couldn't help it. When the bell rang, I was still standing there with this goofy expression on my face. Sabs had to practically drag me off to class.

I sort of just floated through my morning classes. Kids I didn't even know kept congratulating me. Even some of the teachers said something to me.

At lunch, Sabs bought this pink cupcake and stuck a candle in it.

"I wanted to light it, but these guys wouldn't let me," Randy said sullenly.

"Right, Ran," Allison replied. "And get expelled for having matches in school? Forget it!" She shook her head in disbelief.

"Thanks, anyway," I said to Randy.

I was a little bit embarrassed over the big deal they were making. I mean, none of the guys who made the team got cupcakes from their friends with candles in them. I figured this was different, though, since I was the first girl to ever make it.

I cut the cupcake into four pieces and we

each ate one. I felt really good.

I had gym last period that day, which was great because I was too antsy to sit in any more classes. As I was going into the locker room to change, Mrs. O'Neal called me over.

"Congratulations, Katie!" she said with a smile. "So, we finally have a girl on the hockey team. I've been telling Coach Budd to let girls try out for years. You'll be going down in the Bradley Junior High history book, I hope you realize."

I didn't even know they had a Bradley history book. Anyway, I thanked her and jogged back to the locker room.

After school I sat on the lawn. It was a beautiful fall afternoon and I felt like sitting in the sun. Just then Randy showed up.

"What's up?" she asked. She looked really neat in this fuchsia-colored flapper-style dress and a pair of fuchsia cat eyeglasses with rhinestones in the corners hanging around her neck on a chain. She also had on a pair of really thick white socks that were smooshed down around her ankles and a pair of white sneakers.

Before I had a chance to answer, a car horn started honking. It was a brand-new red sportscar, packed with kids in Emily's class. And then Scottie stuck his head out of the back-seat window and waved. My heart started to beat really fast. Scottie was waving at me? I got incredibly excited. But then these two guys I hadn't seen ran down the steps and got in the car.

My stomach sank. I was really glad I hadn't waved back. Who was I kidding, thinking Scottie had waved to me in front of all those eleventh graders?

"So?" Randy asked again.

I told her about Scottie kissing me.

"Scottie Silver kissed you?" Randy repeated, looking really surprised.

"Yeah," I said. "But I think it was a mistake."

"A mistake?" Randy said, and stopped walking. "How do you kiss somebody by mistake? You just happen to pucker up, lean over, and plant one, and then realize that you really meant to punch the person, or something?"

I looked at Randy and started to giggle. Then she started to giggle, and pretty soon we were laughing so hard there were tears in our eyes and we could hardly stand up straight.

"You know," Randy said, when we finally stopped laughing, "what is it you like about that guy, anyway? I mean, besides the fact that he's good-looking?"

"You think he's cute?" I said, surprised.

"Well, kind of..." Randy replied.

I couldn't believe that Randy had admitted she thought Scottie was cute. "I don't know what it is," I said and shrugged. And then I realized that I had just admitted to Randy that I liked him. "What makes you think I like him?" I asked, trying to get out of it.

"Oh, please." Randy snorted. "Everybody knows you have a major thing for him. Every time we talk about him, you turn red."

"Who's everybody?" I asked her in a panic. Did she mean the whole school, including Scottie?

"Well," Randy replied slowly. "Me, and Sabs, and Allison."

"Have you guys been talking about this behind my back?" I asked.

Randy rolled her eyes and didn't say anything. I guess it was a ridiculous question. I mean, if I was one of them, I would have been talking about it, too. Just like at the beginning of the year with Sabs and Alec. We'd all talked that thing to death. I just hoped I hadn't been too obvious about liking Scottie.

"You know," I said when we'd reached Elm Park, where Randy went one way and I went the other. "About those good-looking guys in New York…" I said and let my voice trail off.

Randy laughed. "They're not your type, Katie," she said.

I looked at her. "Maybe, but you never know," I replied.

We both giggled.

Mom was there when I got home. She was sitting on one of the love seats, reading a magazine.

"Hi," I said, taking off my coat. Mom hadn't said anything about hockey for the past few days, but things between us were still sort of weird.

"Katie," Mom said in her serious voice, looking up from her magazine, "I want to talk to you. I've been thinking about what you did," she continued, looking at me. "And although I don't approve of the way you behaved last week, I realize how important hockey is to you."

I didn't say anything. I just stared at her.

"So, if you want to be on the hockey team, then go ahead. I can't say I'm pleased about it, but I don't think I have the right to tell you not to play," she finished.

"Mom, I made the team today," I said, a little sheepishly.

Mom didn't exactly seem glad I made the team, but I could tell she wasn't mad anymore. That was better than nothing. I got up and went over to her and gave her a big kiss on the cheek. She gave me a big hug and she smiled. I smiled, too. These last few weeks had definitely been filled with a lot of firsts.

Chapter Eleven

Scottie calls Katie

SCOTTIE: Hi, can I speak to Katie?

KATIE: Speaking.

SCOTTIE: This is Scottie.

KATIE: Scottie?

SCOTTIE: Yeah, you know, Scottie Silver, from the hockey team.

KATIE: Oh.

SCOTTIE: Well, I was just calling to remind you that the game is at three tomorrow, and you should get there by two-fifteen.

KATIE: I know that. That's what Coach told us at practice the other day.

SCOTTIE: So don't be late. Not that it matters, since it's not like you'll be playing or anything.

KATIE: Thanks a lot!

SCOTTIE: Fine. See you. (He hangs up.)

KATIE: Fine. (At the dial tone.)

Katie calls Sabs

KATIE: Hi, Sabs?

SABRINA: Katie?

KATIE: You'll never believe who just called me!

SABRINA: Who?

KATIE: Scottie.

SABRINA: Scottie Silver! Scottie Silver called you at your house? How'd he get your number? You didn't tell me he asked for your number. I can't believe it!

KATIE: Sabs! He's a jerk! I would never give him my number.

SABRINA: What did he say? Did he say anything about the kiss?

KATIE: This had nothing to do with that! Actually, I don't even know why he called. He knows I know what time the game is.

SABRINA: What are you talking about?

KATIE: That's why he said he called — to remind me what time to be at the rink tomorrow.

SABRINA: Well, what did he say? Tell me exactly what he said.

KATIE: He just said that I should be at the rink by two-fifteen, and then he said that it didn't matter if I was there anyway, because I wouldn't be playing.

SABRINA: Hmmm. That's *all* he said? He didn't say anything else?

KATIE: That was it. And then he hung up.

SABRINA: Well, that's really weird.

KATIE: I know. Listen, Sabs, I have to go. Princess Emily needs the phone.

SABRINA: Okay. I'll talk to you tomorrow morning. Get some sleep.

KATIE: I will. Bye, Sabs.

SABRINA: Bye.

Sabrina calls Allison

SABRINA: Hi. Is Allison home?

CHARLIE: Who?

SABRINA: Your sister, Allison.

CHARLIE: Who?

ALLISON: Hello. This is Allison.

SABRINA: Hi, Al. It's me, Sabs.

ALLISON: Hi, Sabrina.

SABRINA: You'll never believe who called Katie.

ALLISON: Scottie?

SABRINA: How'd you know? How come you always know these things?

ALLISON: I don't know, I just do. So what did he say?

SABRINA: Well, that's just it. He didn't really say anything. He just told Katie to be on time for the game, and then he said it didn't really matter if she showed up at all.

ALLISON: I think he really likes her.

SABRINA: What are you talking about? You're crazy! He was just so mean to her.

ALLISON: Right. He's probably shy....

SABRINA: Scottie Silver? The make-out king?

ALLISON: Yeah, I bet he felt funny calling Katie, so he made up a reason why. And then he was embarrassed, so he was mean to her.

SABRINA: Hmmm. Maybe you're right. I never thought about it that way. You're a genius, Al. Listen, I've got to call Katie right back. Don't forget to remind Randy to meet us at the rink at two-thirty. See you tomorrow. Bye.

ALLISON: Okay. Bye.

Allison calls Randy

ALLISON: Hello. May I speak to Randy, please?

RANDY: You got her.

ALLISON: Oh, hi, Randy. This is Allison.

RANDY: I know. What's going on, Al?

ALLISON: I'm calling to remind you so you don't forget to be at the rink at two-thirty tomorrow.

RANDY: How could I forget? I can't wait to see Katie show all those chauvinists how good a girl can skate. How's she doing anyway? Is she really uptight about it?

ALLISON: She seems pretty calm. I hope she gets to play. Sabrina just called and told me that Scottie just called Katie. I think he might have gotten her a little upset.

RANDY: Trying to psych her out, I bet.

ALLISON: I don't think so, Randy. Actually, I

	think Scottie likes Katie a lot.
RANDY:	That's a possibility. I mean, he did kiss her and all. But that doesn't mean he wants her to do well tomorrow.
ALLISON:	Right. But I don't think he upset her on purpose.
RANDY:	Well, I guess we'll find out. So I'll see you on the flip side.
ALLISON:	Tomorrow?
RANDY:	Right. *Ciao*.
ALLISON:	Good-bye.

Sabrina calls Katie again

SABRINA:	Hi, Emily. This is Sabrina. Is Katie there?
EMILY:	Hold on, I'll get her for you.
KATIE:	What's up, Sabs?
SABRINA:	Are you sitting down? I just got off the phone with Al, and she told me the most incredible thing. You'll never believe it. She said that Scottie Silver like-*likes* you, and that's why he called you.
KATIE:	What are you talking about? He was totally obnoxious. He defi-

nitely doesn't like me. You and Al
don't know what you're talking
about. And anyway, he's going
out with Stacy, isn't he?

SABRINA: So what? It's not like they're
going steady or anything.

KATIE: Well, that's true.

SABRINA: Besides, why else would he call
you?

KATIE: To tell me not to be late tomorrow.
That's what he said, anyway.

SABRINA: Right. But do you think he really
meant that? I mean, come on,
Katie, he knows you know what
time to be there. Maybe he called
for another reason.

KATIE: Like what?

SABRINA: Maybe he called to ask you out
after the game or something.

KATIE: What!

SABRINA: You heard me. I bet that's why he
called you. He wanted to ask you
out. Wow, Katie. That is so totally
unbelievably incredible.

KATIE: You're crazy, Sabs. Look, I've got
to go. Her Royal Highness is wait-

ing for Prince Reed to call. I'll see you tomorrow. Bye.

SABRINA: Katie, I know I'm right. I know about these things. I'll talk to you later. Bye.

Chapter Twelve

On Saturday I was kind of jumpy about the game, so I called Sabs to see if I could come to her house for a while. Her dog Cinnamon had just had puppies and I wanted to see them.

When I got to her house the front door was open so I knocked and went in.

"Katie, is that you?" Sabs called.

"Yeah, where are you?" I called back.

"In the kitchen," she said.

Sabs was breaking some eggs into a bowl. I sat down at the kitchen table and suddenly realized how hungry I was.

"Want some eggs?" Sabs asked as she wiped her hands on her jeans.

"No, thanks," I said, making a face. "Do you have any cereal?"

"You know where everything is," Sabs said, shrugging.

I went into the pantry. There were about ten

different kinds of cereal in there. I picked a really sugary one. My mother only buys bran flakes and shredded wheat and boring stuff like that.

After we finished eating, Sabs took me to see the puppies. They were in Sam and Mark's room, in the closet. Cinnamon sleepily opened one eye when she heard us come in, and then closed it. The puppies were so cute.

"Mom said to offer you one," Sabs whispered to me as we stood there staring at the puppies.

"Oh, I'd love one," I replied. "But you know how my mother is."

"Yeah," Sabs agreed. "So we decided, Mom and Dad and my brothers and me, that you get to name the little gray one. You can pretend he's yours, only he'll live with us."

"You're kidding!" I exclaimed. Impulsively I leaned over and hugged Sabs. "You're the best," I said.

At one o'clock I went home to get ready for the big game. I was glad I'd spent the morning with Sabs. At least it had taken my mind off things for a while.

When I got to the rink, I went straight to the coach's office. He'd arranged for me to change there since the visitors' locker room was being used.

"See you in ten minutes," he said, rising from his desk. "And good luck out there, Katie." I smiled. Coach Budd wasn't as tough as he seemed.

"Now," I heard the coach say as I walked into the boys' locker room, "I'm sure that all of you know that Valley is one of the best teams in the state. Some of you remember playing them last year. But after watching all of you in practice, I know you're just as good, even better. So go out there, and play your hearts out." Then he stood up, and raised his voice. "Let's go out there and get 'em!"

Everybody went running out of the locker room, but I sort of lagged behind. There was this diagram on the blackboard that I guessed all of the other guys had already seen, detailing our strategy for the game. I figured it wasn't really important that I look at it, since I probably wouldn't be playing. But I did, anyway, and got the basic defensive strategy.

The game was going pretty well. Valley got

off to a good start, but we were looking good, too. The crowd was roaring. Scottie, Brian, Flip, and three other guys were in the starting line-up. Even though I wasn't even playing, I still felt pretty cool sitting on the bench in my uniform with the rest of the team. I couldn't help but wonder if Mom and Emily had come to the game.

During half time, I went and sat by myself in the coach's office. I'd never felt so strange before. Like I belonged and didn't belong all at the same time. About five minutes before we had to go back out on the ice, the coach called me back into the locker room with everyone in order to go over more plays.

About fifteen minutes into the last period, the score was tied 1-1. Brian had the puck, and he was stick-handling it, side to side, when a defensiveman came up next to him and tried to poke-check the puck. Somehow Brian's blade got caught in the stock, and he went flying across the ice and slammed into the boards. He didn't get up right away. The ref blew his whistle, and the trainer shuffled out onto the ice. He helped Brian up, but everyone could see that he was hurt. He was definitely going to be out of the game. Now what were we going to do? Brian was the only left wing. And then it hit me. Left wing was the position the coach kept making me play during our practice sessions.

The next thing I knew, the coach was calling my number to get out on the ice. He didn't look too thrilled about it, either.

Somehow I managed to put my helmet on and get out there. I was petrified, until the whistle blew and we started to play. Valley had the puck, so I didn't get near it for a couple of minutes. The other guys on our team were really covering for me. I guessed they didn't think I could cut it out there.

And then, with one minute left and the score still tied, I got the puck!

The center from Valley was open, and without even thinking about it, I just poke-checked that puck. Somehow the center leaned too far forward and lost his balance. I took the puck and skated away. In one second the defensivemen were on me, but I saw Scottie out of the corner of my eye and he was open. So I faked a pass to my left and, being a fast skater, I was able to cut away to my right, where Scottie was free. He rushed up the ice, with me right behind him. I headmanned the puck to him, and before the other team even knew what was happening, he hit a slap shot that went right past the goalie and into the net. Then the bell sounded. We'd won the game!

All of the guys from our team came out onto the ice and crowded around me. Flip and Brian picked me up on their shoulders. Everyone was chanting, "Katie! Katie! Katie!" Even the coach was beaming. And that's when I looked up in the stands and saw Mom and Emily. They were both clapping, and Emily was actually jumping up and down. I couldn't believe it.

I still had this incredible feeling inside as I walked to the coach's office. I could barely get all of my pads off because I was shaking so much. I had to hang around for a while, since Valley was still using the visitors' locker room and I wanted to take a shower. I kept replaying the winning moves in my mind.

"Katie," the coach called as he knocked on the door.

"Yeah?" I replied, coming back to earth. "Come in!"

"The locker room's all clear," he said,

putting his clipboard down on his desk.

I picked up my stuff and headed for the door.

"Katie," the coach said.

I turned around.

"You did a fine job out there. You really pulled for the team," he said with a smile. "I knew I picked a winner when I picked you."

My mouth dropped open in shock. I'd assumed I'd only made the team because the coach was afraid of getting into legal problems if he didn't let me play, or something. I couldn't believe he actually thought I was good.

"Thank you," I said and smiled back at him.

I was practically floating when I got to the locker room. I took a nice hot shower and then got dressed. I'd brought a pair of jeans with me and one of Emily's nicest sweaters. The sweater had been sitting on my bed when I got back from Sabs's that afternoon. I guess it was Emily's idea of a peace offering. I was happy about it, since Sabs, Randy, Allison, and I were all going to Fitzie's after the game, and I wanted to look nice.

I was on my way out the door when I saw Scottie.

We just stood there, looking at each other.

"You were great out there today," Scottie said softly. "You won the game for us. Thanks."

I smiled, but didn't say anything. I couldn't.

"Um…" Scottie began. "About last night on the phone…" He stopped and I just looked at him. "Well, I'm sorry that I was kind of obnoxious."

"That's okay," I said quickly.

Scottie shifted from foot to foot, his hands jammed in his pockets. "Do you…um…want to…uh…go to Fitzie's with me?" he finally asked. "For a soda or something?"

"I can't," I said quickly. "I mean…I'd…uh …love to, but I'm going to Fitzie's with my friends." I pointed to Sabs, Randy, and Allison, who were standing there waiting for me. I was in shock. I couldn't believe that Scottie Silver had actually asked me out.

Sabs took one look at Scottie and me and knew what to do. "Katie, we'll go on ahead — see you at Fitzie's," she said.

"Yeah. See you in a few minutes," Allison and Randy chimed in.

I smiled gratefully at them. Suddenly I noticed that Stacy, Eva, Laurel, and B.Z. had appeared. They were standing right behind Scottie.

"Scottie," Stacy whined. "Aren't you ready?"

Scottie didn't even turn around. He just looked at me. "I'll catch you there, Stacy," he replied.

"Let's get out of here," Stacy said, sneering, and she and her clones stormed away.

"Well," Allison said, "we'll see you at Fitzie's, Katie." Randy winked at me and elbowed Sabs, who was still standing there wide-eyed.

Scottie bent down to pick up my gear, but I stopped him. I picked it up myself.

"I can handle it," I said, and we both laughed.

Titles in the GIRL TALK series

LOOK FOR THE GIRL TALK BOOKS!
COMING SOON TO A BOOKSTORE NEAR YOU!

LOOK FOR THESE GIRL TALK GAMES AND PRODUCTS!

Girl Talk Games:
- Girl Talk Game
- Girl Talk Second Edition
- Girl Talk Travel Game
- Girl Talk Date Line

Girl Talk Puzzles:
- Hunk
- Heart to Heart

The Girl Talk Collection:
- Blushers
- Lip Gloss
- Hair Fashions
- 20 Anywhere Stickers
- Slumber Party Kit
- Eye Shadow
- Fingernails
- Paints that Puff
- Fantasy Fortune Party Kit

TALK BACK!

TELL US WHAT YOU THINK ABOUT GIRL TALK

Name _Karen Smith_

Address _2 Diaz St._

City _E. Haven_ State _CT_ Zip _06513_

Birthday: Day _21_ Mo _1_ Year _82_

Telephone Number (_203_) _467-5656_

1) On a scale of 1 (The Pits) to 5 (The Max), how would you rate Girl Talk?   Circle One:

1 2 3 4 (5)

2) What do you like most about Girl Talk?

___Characters___Situations___Telephone Talk

Other _____

3) Who is your favorite character?   Circle One:

(Sabrina)   Katie   Randy

Allison   Stacy   Other

4) Who is your least favorite character?

Stacy

5) What do you want to read about in Girl Talk?

romantic stuff

Send completed form to :
Western Publishing Company, Inc.
1220 Mound Avenue Mail Station #85
Racine, Wisconsin 53404